The Coming of the SCORPION!

VISIT US AT
www.abdopub.com

Spotlight, a division of ABDO Publishing Company Inc., is the school and library distributor of the Marvel Entertainment books.

Library bound edition © 2006

Library of Congress Cataloging-in-Publication Data

The Coming of the Scorpion!

ISBN 1-59961-018-3   (Reinforced Library Bound Edition)

All Spotlight books are reinforced library binding and manufactured in the United States of America

See ya, Liz. We'll study together for the history test tomorrow.

Get lost, *Parker*. Liz doesn't need *your* help on the test.

Quiet, Flash.

Sounds cool, Peter. And *thanks again* for helping me out.

"And thanks again for helping me out."

Geez, Liz, *I* could help you study.

Yeah--

--if I wanted a *D average*.

I *could* get better grades. I just don't want everyone thinkin' I'm a geek, like Parker.

Well, then you're *dumber* than I thought.

Near the Parker residence...

What's up with my spider-sense?

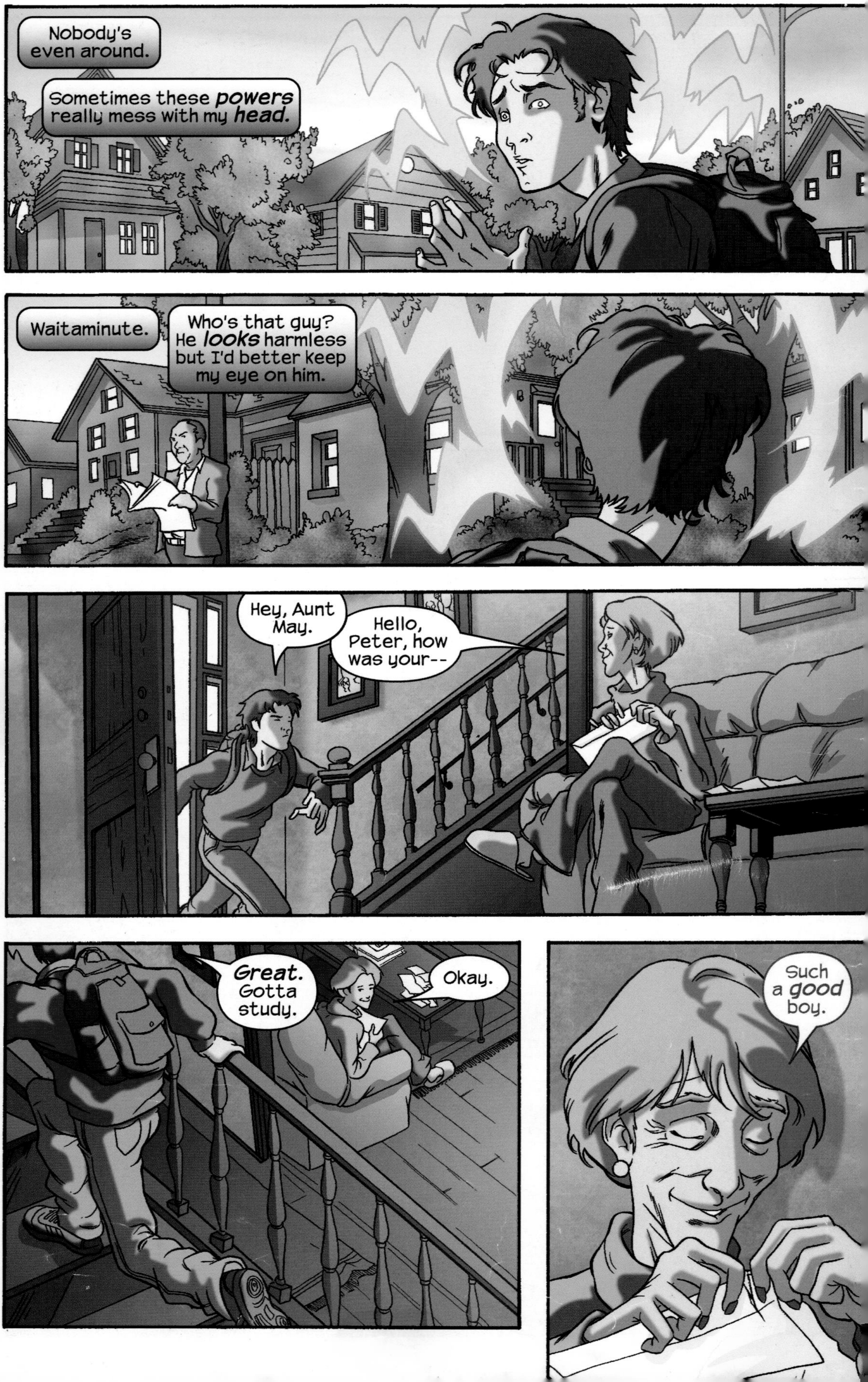
Nobody's even around.
Sometimes these powers really mess with my head.
Waitaminute.
Who's that guy? He looks harmless but I'd better keep my eye on him.
Hey, Aunt May.
Hello, Peter, how was your--
Great. Gotta study.
Okay.
Such a good boy.

He's *watching* the house.

What if he's figured out that I'm Spider-Man?

He's going. *Finally.*

Well, it's time to change from the hunted--

--to the *hunter.*

Man, I am getting *way* too into this super-hero stuff.

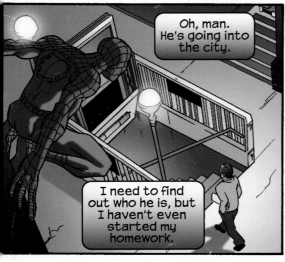

Oh, man. He's going into the city.

I need to find out who he is, but I haven't even started my homework.

How am I supposed to be a big super hero when I have to make time for an English essay?

KNOCK KNOCK

Come on in.

So what do you have for me, MacGargan?

Did you see how *Parker* gets all those *great shots* of Spider-Man?

Did you follow Spider-Man back to his *lair*?

Lair, sir?

Of course. All these *creepy vigilante types* have lairs.

Sure. I mean, *NO*, Parker didn't take any shots of Spider-Man today.

Well, stop by tomorrow afternoon. I have this thing I wanted to check out and I thought you'd like to come along.

Sure thing, Jonah. You're the boss.

Dr. Farley Stillwell

Science Fiction-- or FACT?

Hi, Peter.

Hey, Betty.

Is Mr. Jameson in? I was hoping to pick up an assignment.

He's *in*, but he's got someone with him right now.

I've never seen the guy before, but he's not a reporter or anything.

Hey, are you okay?

My boyfriend is going away for three months to Europe.

Your boyfriend? I didn't even know you had a boyfriend...

I'm sorry.

Betty, what's wrong? Did Parker say something--?

No, Mr. Jameson. I'm sorry. He was *consoling* me.

That's the guy who was *following* me the other night!

What's he doing with Mr. Jameson?!

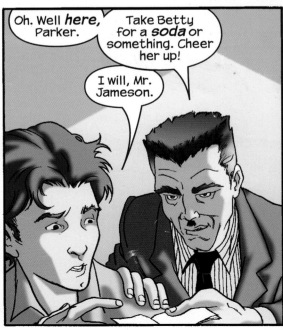

Oh. Well *here,* Parker. Take Betty for a *soda* or something. Cheer her up!

I will, Mr. Jameson.

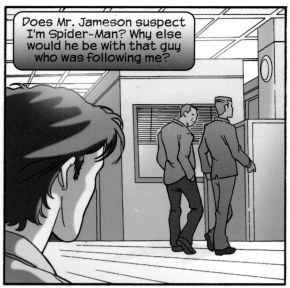

Does Mr. Jameson suspect I'm Spider-Man? Why else would he be with that guy who was following me?

Thanks for talking with me, Peter.

Billy and I have never been apart this long...

Uh-- sure.

I'd follow them, but I can't just ditch Betty.

It's been awhile since we've hung out.

It has. I miss our talks. You've just seemed so busy with school and taking photos and--

Well, I should make time for you.

You've been *nothing* but *nice* to me. You're one of the only people who always has been.

Thanks, Peter.

I don't mean to be a bother--

Betty, it's *no* bother.

Believe me. I should enjoy the quiet time with you.

Oh, like your life is so crazy. *Mr. Excitement* over here...

You have *no* idea, Betty.

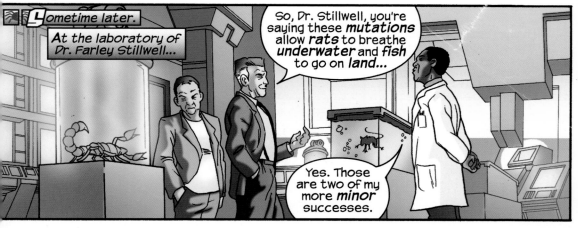

Sometime later.

At the laboratory of Dr. Farley Stillwell...

So, Dr. Stillwell, you're saying these *mutations* allow *rats* to breathe *underwater* and *fish* to go on *land*...

Yes. Those are two of my more *minor* successes.

What would your experiments do for a *human being*?

The government does not allow that kind of testing.

TAP

TAP

They believe me to be a modern-day Dr. Frankenstein, I'm afraid.

Please stop tapping on the glass.

The experiment seems to make the animals more *aggressive* than they would normally be.

Yeah, he's a touchy little thing.

Given the opportunity, would you be able to give a person abilities as great as Spider-Man's?

I just told you, the government is *shutting* me *down*.

And they wouldn't *approve* of--

Hypothetically speaking...

Well, I suppose that, *hypothetically*--

--I could *probably* create a combination of *strength* and *agility* that would *surpass* Spider-Man's abilities.

What if *I* provided you with the funding to carry on your experiments?

And what if the government *never* needed to *know* what *happened* here *today*?

Mr. Jameson, I'm not sure if you're the *ideal* subject.

Oh no. *I'm* not going to do it.

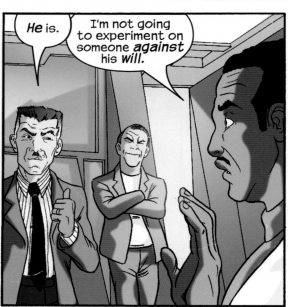

He is.

I'm not going to experiment on someone *against* his *will*.

Hey *Doc,* I'm getting *paid* exactly like *you.*

If the man wants a *guinea pig,* just tell me where to squeal.

This *check* might clear up any *lingering* doubts.

Now, *that* is a *persuasive argument,* Mr. Jameson.

I *thought* it might be.

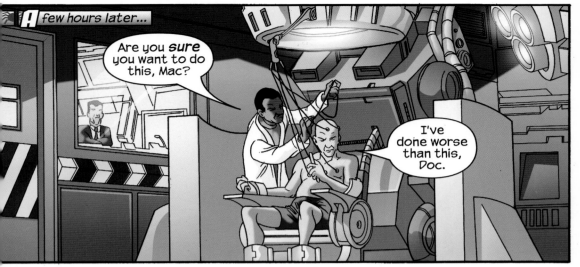

Are you *sure* you want to do this, Mac?

I've done worse than this, Doc.

Well, *drink up* and we'll start the procedure.

If you feel *anything*--

If I feel anything *strange*, Doc, I'll let you know.

Ick. That was pretty *nasty stuff.*

All right. Here we go.

Hey Doc... this feels *amazing!*

Keep it coming!

Is it working?

It's going *better* than I could have hoped.

He's already gaining muscle mass...

...using the Scorpion DNA seems to be the key to success!

That's *it.* He should now be ten times as strong as he was...

...and his reflexes should be heightened.

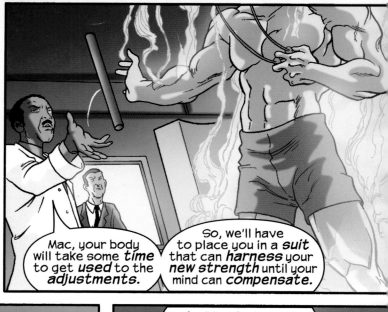

Mac, your body will take some *time* to get *used* to the *adjustments*.

So, we'll have to place you in a *suit* that can *harness* your *new strength* until your mind can *compensate*.

CRREEEK!

Will he be *strong enough* to defeat Spider-Man?

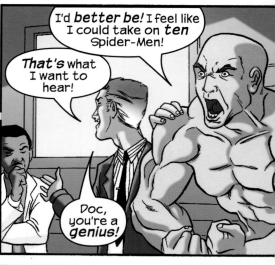

I'd *better be!* I feel like I could take on *ten* Spider-Men!

That's what I want to hear!

Doc, you're a *genius!*

I need to run a few *tests* so I can *compare* the *data*--

--but after that the two of you will be *free to go.*

Perfect. Now all we need is for *Spider-Man* to come into the *open* so *Mac* can take him *down.*

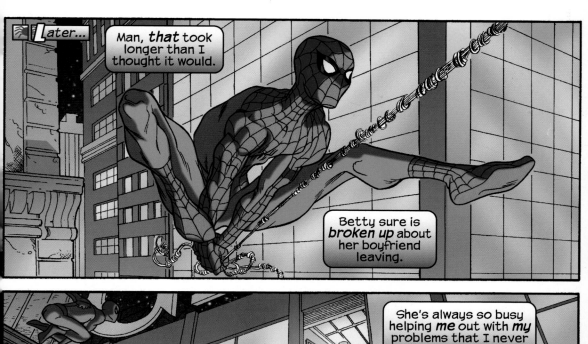

Man, *that* took longer than I thought it would.

Betty sure is *broken up* about her boyfriend leaving.

She's always so busy helping *me* out with *my* problems that I never think to ask about *hers.*

I need to stop being so *focused* on myself.

Hey, Jonah's back in his office.

Now's as good a time as *any* to find out what the deal was with the guy *following* me.

THWIP

Hey, *grumpy.* What's got you *working* so late?

Spider-Man!

CALUMET CITY PUBLIC LIBRARY

Just the man I wanted to see.

Why don't you come on in and *sit down.* Let's do an *exclusive* right here.

Maybe we can clear up some of our *problems* and *start fresh.*

Yeah, *right!* You call me a *menace* for *months* and then you just want to *chat?* No thanks.

Spider-Man, *wait!* I have someone who--

--wants to meet you.

Spidey-sense is really banging away.

Waitaminute-- is Jonah setting me up?!

Gotcha, wall-crawler!

Yeah-- definitely a set-up...

CRASH!

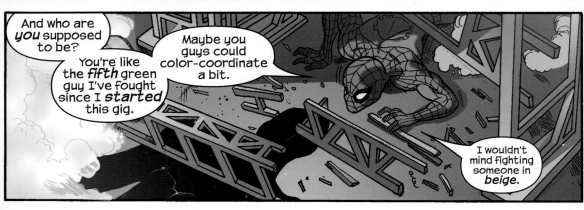

And who are *you* supposed to be? You're like the *fifth* green guy I've fought since I *started* this gig.

Maybe you guys could color-coordinate a bit.

I wouldn't mind fighting someone in *beige*.

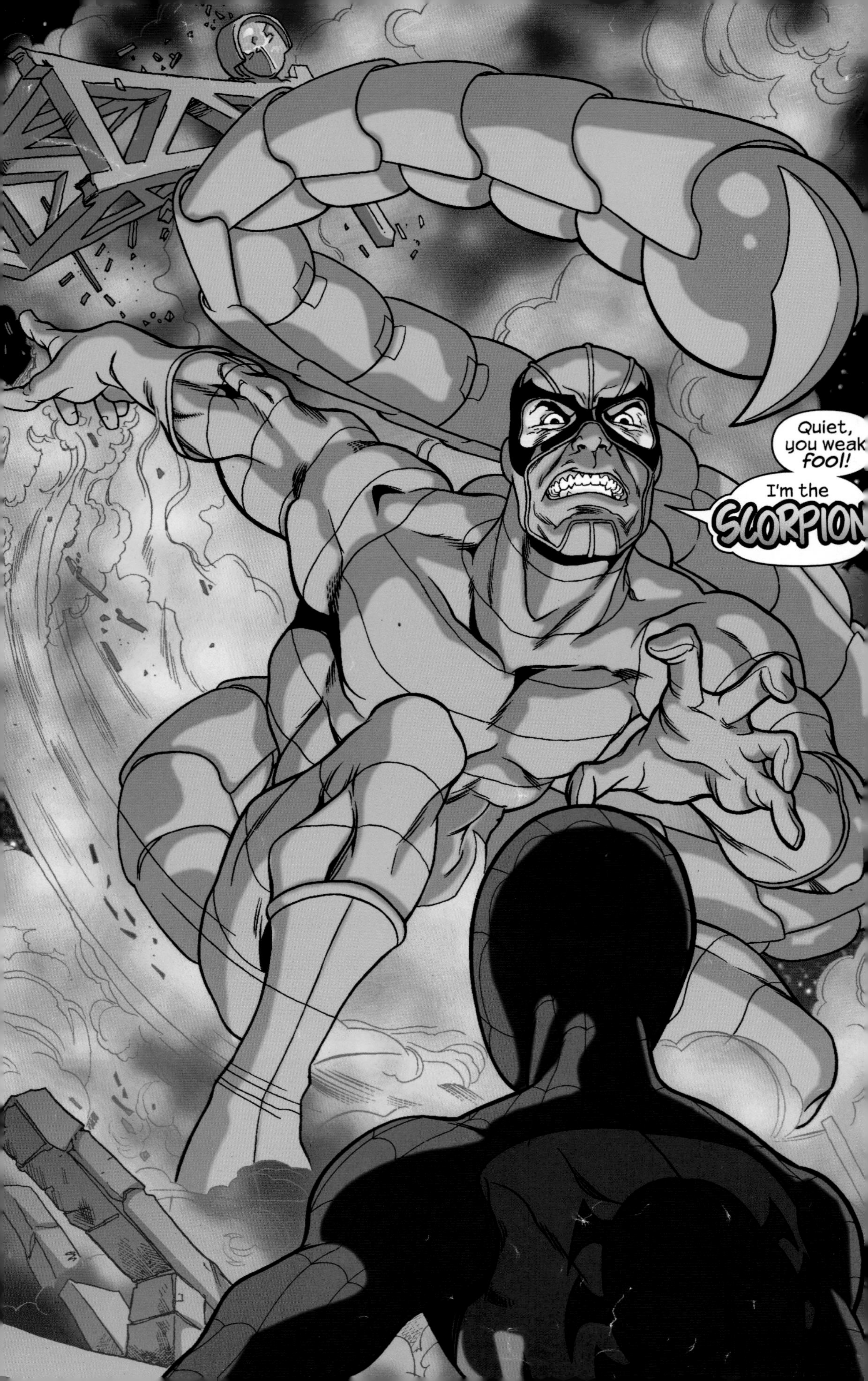
Quiet, you weak fool!
I'm the SCORPION!

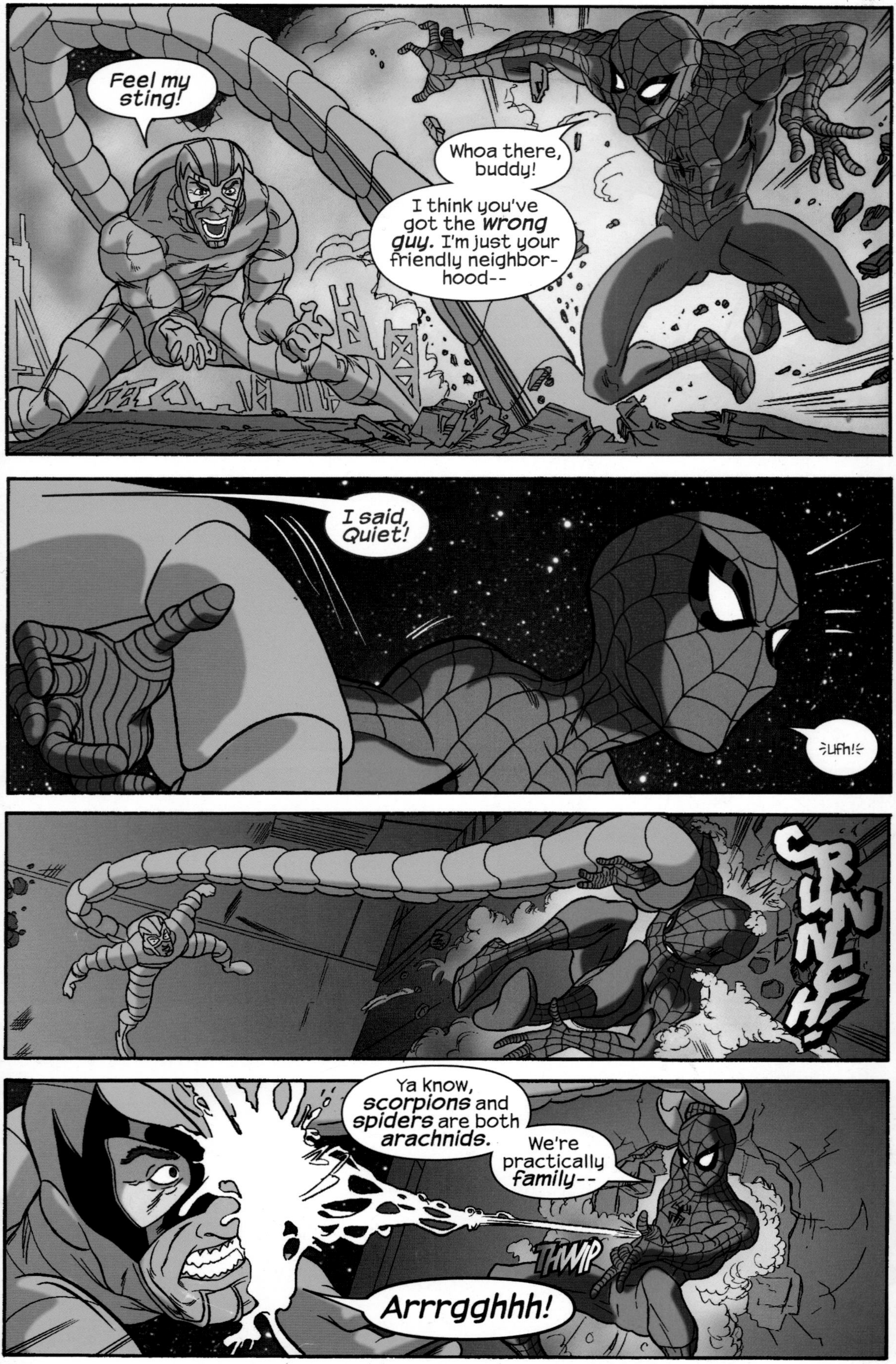
Feel my sting!
Whoa there, buddy!
I think you've got the wrong guy. I'm just your friendly neighbor-hood--
I said, Quiet!
UFH!
CRUNCH!
Ya know, scorpions and spiders are both arachnids.
We're practically family--
THWIP
Arrrgghhh!

--but, I don't suppose that changes anything. Does it, Scorpy?

These webs may be strong enough to hold normal men--

--but I'm anything *but* normal now.

≲uhhh≳

Finally! Someone *man enough* to take down Spider-Man!

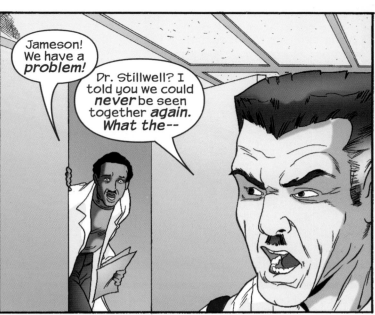

Jameson! We have a *problem!*

Dr. Stillwell? I told you we could *never* be seen together *again.* What the--

This *couldn't wait!*

MacGargan--his mind--the experiment may have different *side effects* than I imagined.

What's it *matter* as long as it's a *success?*

You're a *genius!*

No. I'm *not.*

He's *stronger* than *Spider-Man.* Take a look out this window.

I never worried about it *before* because I only worked on *animals,* but the process does something to the *subject's mind.*

Remember the *rat* that *lunged* at you?

"The data shows that Mac's *brain cells* are *disintegrating*.

"The more he *exerts himself*, the more his *brain* will *fry*. He's losing his *mind*.

I was hoping we could settle this over a game of rock, paper, scissors...

You think you can defeat me, Spider-Man?

"He's going to become more and more aggressive until he's running on pure emotion. Pure *hate!*

Okay. You win. No more joking.

Can you please stop crushing me now?

Quit *joking around!* You can't beat me! *No one can!*

"Who knows what he's going to do after he *takes out* Spider-Man! His mind could *give way* completely!

RAAAHHH!

Um, ouch!

SMASSHH!

"Who knows who could be *hurt* by his *insanity!*"

You never told me *this* could happen, Stillwell!

Well, I think I can *stall* the *process*. And if I can revert him to *normal*, even if for a short time, I can try to *cure* him.

I just need to *inject* him with *this*.

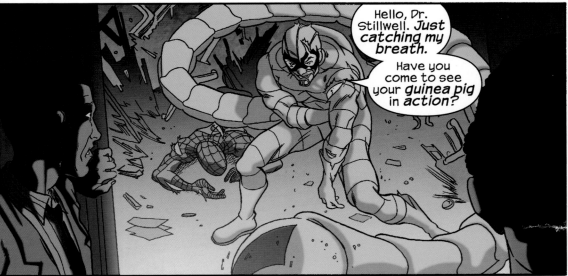

Hello, Dr. Stillwell. *Just catching my breath.*

Have you come to see your *guinea pig* in *action*?

MacGargan--

Call me *The Scorpion*, Doc.

I like the *sound of that*, don't you?

You *have* to let me help you before it's *too late*.

If we don't give you this serum, your mind will slip away--

--you'll be left with nothing but animal instinct.

I'm losing my mind?

Then I can't be held *responsible* for my actions, can I?

Maybe *you'll* be my *first victim* instead of Spider-Man.

You think you can *give* me this power and then take it *away*?

NO!

Violence is *never* the answer, big-guy-in-a-suit-worse-than-mine!

And it sounds like *you two* have some *emotional healing* to do...

I know. I hate shots too.

Get off me, Spider-Man!

But it's for your own good.

Just look the other way...

NO!

THUNK!

No! Don't take away--

--my power...

THUMP!

You all right, sir?

Yes, Spider-Man.

You did this to him?

Yes. But I didn't know...

I'm not sure if the serum will remove his powers permanently--

--but it might give me a chance to help him.

Don't let it happen again, Doc.

Someone could get hurt...

Well, besides me that is.

I won't, Spider-Man. And I'll figure out a *cure* for his *madness*.

Spider-Man, you wall-crawling *creep!*

Look at all the *damage* you caused to that *building!*

You should turn yourself in!

THWIP

Give it a rest, Jameson.

Smimiermam! Guhhagheere!

And leave the dressing-up-as-an-arachnid to the professionals.

The end